The Star-Spangled Banner

Edited by Barbie H. Schwaeber

Illustrated by Frank Ordaz

SMITHSONIAN INSTITUTION

Book design: Konrad Krukowski
Editor: Barbie Heit Schwaeber
Production Editor: Brian E. Giblin

First Edition 2007
10 9 8 7 6 5 4 3 2 1
Printed in China

Acknowledgments:
    Our very special thanks to Marilyn Zoidis of Smithsonian's National Museum of American History, Behring Center for her curatorial review of this title.
    Soundprints would also like to thank Ellen Nanney and Katie Mann at the Smithsonian Institution's Office of Product Development and Licensing for their help in the creation of this book.

O' say can you see, by the dawn's early light,

What so proudly we hail'd
at the twilight's last gleaming,

Whose broad stripes and bright stars
through the perilous fight

And the rocket's red glare,

The bombs bursting in air,

Gave proof through the night

that our flag was still there,

O' say does that star-spangled banner yet wave

**O'er the land of the free
and the home of the brave?**

Notes and Nostalgia

"The Star-Spangled Banner" was written by Francis Scott Key during the Battle of Baltimore in 1814. This battle was one of several major battles that occurred between British and American forces during the War of 1812.

Francis Scott Key was born on August 1, 1779, in Frederick, Maryland, and spent his boyhood growing up on a plantation called Terra Rubra. He was raised to be a well-educated man who was very committed to his family and his country. His father, John Ross Key, was a judge who fought in the American Revolution and taught his son and daughter, Anne, about the history of the United States. It was his family's influence that helped Francis develop his lifelong religious faith and his love of poetry.

Francis attended St. John's Grammar School in Annapolis, and later St. John's College, where he graduated with honors at age seventeen. After graduating from college, he went on to study law. He then met his future wife, Mary Tayloe Lloyd, or Polly as he called her. The couple eventually settled in Georgetown and raised a large family. Francis Scott Key died in Baltimore, Maryland, on January 11, 1843.

When he wrote "The Star-Spangled Banner," Francis Scott Key was working as an attorney in Washington, D.C. He was called away from his busy law practice to aid his family friend, Dr. William Beanes, who was being held prisoner aboard a British military ship at sea. Key was able to negotiate the release of Beanes, but the Americans were not able to leave the harbor. Forced to wait on a small boat, the men witnessed the attack on Fort McHenry which began at 6:30 a.m. on September 13, 1814 and continued for 25 long hours. Rockets glared and bombs burst through the air as Key watched in fear, wondering what would become of the American fort. When dawn broke, the smoke began to clear and a slight breeze began to blow. That's when Key was able to finally spot the U.S. flag flying over Fort McHenry—which meant that the U.S. had won the battle!

The events that Key witnessed and experienced during those 25 hours inspired him to write the poem that eventually became "The Star-Spangled Banner." In fact, he began writing the poem while still at sea. As he wrote the poem, he had the tune of a popular British song in mind. The song was called "To Anacreon in Heaven." When it was completed, Key's poem had four verses. The first verse is the one we sing today.

After the Battle of Fort McHenry, Francis Scott Key returned to Baltimore. Anxious and exhausted from the events that he had witnessed, he went straight to the Indian Queen Hotel on Baltimore Street for some much-needed rest and finished the poem in his hotel room.

He showed the poem to his brother-in-law, Judge Joseph H. Nicholson who eagerly took the poem to the newspaper office of the *Baltimore American*, where the verses were set in type and printed. First named "The Defence [sic] of Fort McHenry" the poem and song were soon renamed "The Star-Spangled Banner." After its first publication in Baltimore, the song was printed and sung in many cities across the country. "The Star-Spangled Banner" was officially adopted by the U.S. Navy in 1889 to accompany the raising and lowering of the flag.

On March 3, 1931, more than a century after the song was written, President Herbert Hoover signed a document making the "The Star-Spangled Banner" the country's national anthem! Today, the song is sung at official ceremonies, schools and sporting events, including the Olympic Games every time an American athlete wins a gold medal, to show pride, loyalty and respect for our country. The actual flag that inspired the song is on display at the Smithsonian's National Museum of American History in Washington, D.C.

The Star-Spangled Banner

Lyrics by Francis Scott Key

Music by John Stafford Smith

Although we sing only the first verse today, Francis Scott Key originally wrote four verses of "The Star-Spangled Banner." Here is the original song as it appears in the Maryland Historical Society's collection:

The Star-Spangled Banner

O' say can you see, by the dawn's early light,
What so proudly we hail'd at the twilight's last gleaming,
Whose broad stripes and bright stars through the perilous fight
O'er the ramparts we watch'd were so gallantly streaming?
And the rocket's red glare, the bomb bursting in air,
Gave proof through the night that our flag was still there,
O say does that star-spangled banner yet wave
O'er the land of the free and the home of the brave?

On the shore dimly seen through the mists of the deep
Where the foe's haughty host in dread silence reposes,
What is that which the breeze, o'er the towering steep,
As it fitfully blows, half conceals, half discloses?
Now it catches the gleam of the morning's first beam,
In full glory reflected now shines in the stream,
'Tis the star-spangled banner — O long may it wave
O'er the land of the free and the home of the brave!

And where is that band who so vauntingly swore,
That the havoc of war and the battle's confusion
A home and a Country should leave us no more?
Their blood has wash'd out their foul footstep's pollution.
No refuge could save the hireling and slave
From the terror of flight or the gloom of the grave,
And the star-spangled banner in triumph doth wave
O'er the land of the free and the home of the brave.

O' thus be it ever when freemen shall stand
Between their lov'd home and the war's desolation!
Blest with vict'ry and peace may the heav'n rescued land
Praise the power that hath made and preserv'd us a nation!
Then conquer we must, when our cause it is just,
And this be our motto — "In God is our trust,"
And the star-spangled banner in triumph shall wave
O'er the land of the free and the home of the brave.